DISNEY'S
THE
LION KING
MORNING AT PRIDE ROCK

BY Teddy Slater

ILLUSTRATED BY Robbin Cuddy AND David Pacheco

Disney PRESS
NEW YORK

FIRST EDITION
3 5 7 9 10 8 6 4

Library of Congress Catalog Card Number: 93-74741
ISBN 1-56282-690-5/1-56282-691-3 (lib. bdg.)

Disney's
THE
LION KING
MORNING AT PRIDE ROCK

A hot orange sun lights the African sky.

A new day is about to begin.

*T*he tawny cheetah pricks up her ears.
She hears a soft whisper. She hears a sweet sigh.

Something is calling her on the wind,
calling her to Pride Rock.

A mother rhinoceros sniffs the warm breeze.

She can almost taste the excitement.

Curious meerkats turn toward the east, searching the vast empty plain.

Zazu the hornbill urges them on.

*I*n the still of the morning, storks plod through a pool.

Their journey has barely begun.

*W*ith a sudden explosion of motion and sound,

elephants trumpet the news....

*T*here's a great whoosh of wings, and the sky blazes pink

A wave of flamingos flies by.

*B*lack-and-white zebras follow below,

trotting across the savannah.

A family of monkeys runs to keep up.

They don't want to be left behind.

Graceful gazelles kick up their heels,

their hooves barely touching the ground.

An elegant herd of giraffes lopes along.

They stretch their long necks toward Pride Rock.

*H*igh on a hill, topi wonder and wait.

They sense that the moment is near.

On Pride Rock, the Lion King waits with the queen while the animals gather below.

Mufasa and Sarabi sit tall and proud.
A golden cub sleeps at their side.

The great mystic Rafiki, Mufasa's dear friend,

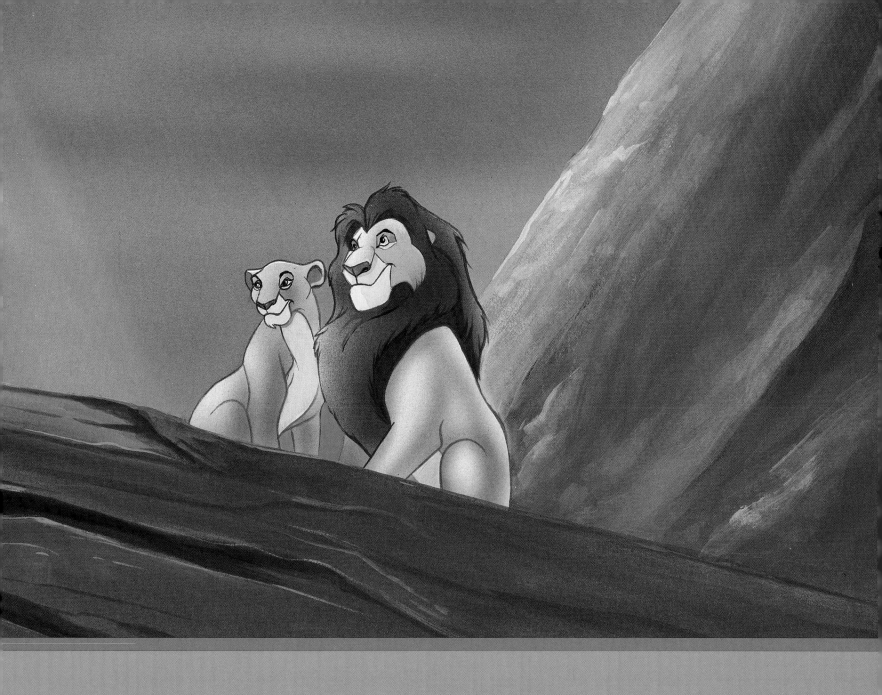

proudly presents the king's son.

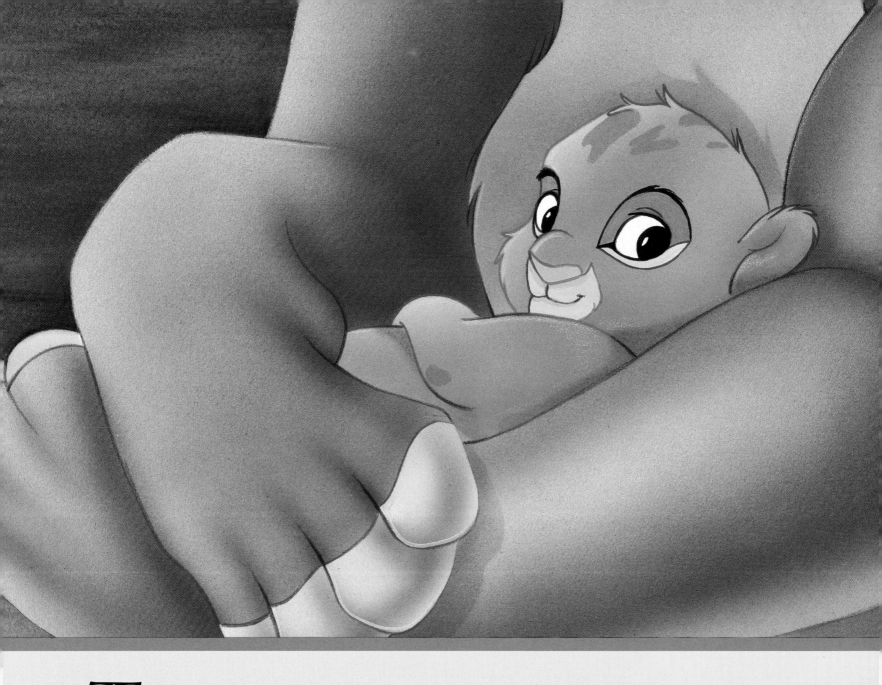

*T*he Lion Prince, Simba, is born.